For information address Disney Press,
1101 Flower Street, Glendale, California 91201.

Printed in China
First Edition
3 5 7 9 10 8 6 4 2
ISBN 978-1-4847-0287-1
T425-2382-5-14356

For more Disney Press fun, visit www.disneybooks.com
This book was printed on paper created from a sustainable source.

# Tiana
## and the Jewel
## of the Bayou

DISNEP PRESS

New York • Los Angeles

One summer morning, Tiana, Naveen, Eudora, and Charlotte were discussing party plans. Tiana's birthday was just days away!

Naveen was worried. Although he had spent weeks looking, he still hadn't found the perfect gift for his princess. And now time was running out!

The prince had looked at everything, from priceless paintings to fine French perfume to beautiful silk and lace.

But he had always come home empty-handed. Nothing seemed special enough for Princess Tiana.

Exhausted, the prince plopped himself into a chair.

Luckily, the following day,
Naveen overheard Tiana speaking with
Charlotte in the kitchen.

"When my daddy and I used to go fishing in the bayou,
we'd sometimes find a piece of swamp amber," said Tiana.
"I thought it was the most precious thing in all the world!"

"That's it!" whispered Naveen, and he dashed out the door.

Naveen met up with the jazz-loving alligator Louis. The two of them went to ask Mama Odie if she could help them find some swamp amber.

"You don't need my help!" said Mama Odie, laughing. "Go find it yourself. You know what to do."

As the birthday party was about to begin, Tiana couldn't find Naveen anywhere. Then one of the guests said he had seen the prince down by the old, mossy tree in the bayou.

Eudora and Charlotte told Tiana not to worry. But Tiana was afraid Naveen might be in trouble.

Tiana ran down to the river and
climbed into a rowboat.

As she rowed into the bayou, she saw Naveen in
the distance. He was diving into the water at the base
of the old tree. Louis was on the bank trying to get a
thorn out of his foot.

"Naveen!" Tiana called out. When the prince didn't resurface, she removed the sashes and petticoats from her dress and dove into the water!

She found Naveen in a tangle of roots. He motioned to her that he was fine, but Tiana grabbed his hand and pulled him to the surface.

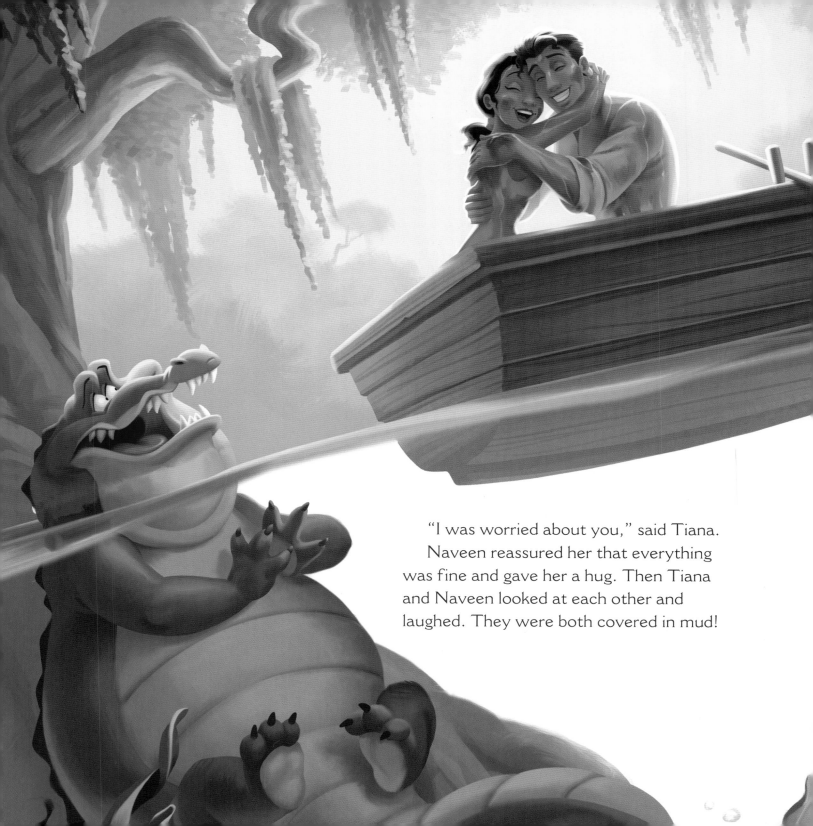

"I was worried about you," said Tiana. Naveen reassured her that everything was fine and gave her a hug. Then Tiana and Naveen looked at each other and laughed. They were both covered in mud!

Naveen opened his hand to reveal a plain, muddy rock. "I'm a little embarrassed," he said. "I was expecting a sparkling jewel, but this is just . . ."

"Swamp amber!" Tiana exclaimed. "What a wonderful birthday surprise!"

When Tiana and Naveen returned to the party, the guests gasped at the sight of them.

Then Charlotte saw the birthday gift and screamed in fright. But Tiana explained that the muddy rock brought back wonderful, loving memories of her daddy. "That is the most precious gift of all," said Tiana. "And now that Naveen is here with me, I couldn't ask for anything more."

As the prince and princess went to change their clothes, Mama Odie picked up the swamp amber. "A little sparkle couldn't hurt," she said, tossing the rock into a pot of gumbo. "Gumbo, gumbo in the pot, we need some sparkle. What you got?"

In a puff of magic, the swamp amber
became a dazzling golden jewel set in
a fine necklace.

"Mama Odie!" Naveen exclaimed.
"How did you do that?"

Mama Odie winked at Tiana. "Oh, it's just a talent we have down here in the bayou. We like to take things that are a little slimy and rough around the edges and turn 'em into something wonderful!"

Tiana smiled. "Like turning crawfish into gumbo!" she said.

"Or a frog into a prince!" Naveen agreed as he took his beautiful princess in his arms, and they danced the night away.